Wrong Number

by

Chloë Rayban

Published in 2004 in Great Britain by
Barrington Stoke Ltd, Sandeman House, Trunk's Close,
55 High Street, Edinburgh EH1 1SR

ISBN 1-842992-00-7

Printed in Great Britain by Bell & Bain Ltd

A Note from the Author

There are times when you think nothing is going to happen to you – *ever*. Everyone you know seems to be having a life, while yours is about as thrilling as soggy Weetabix. Then suddenly, quite out of the blue, some chance event changes your life completely.

This is what happened to Marie when she answered a call on her mobile. It was a wrong number, but was it the *right* boy?

This story actually happened, for real, to someone I know. What happened to the boy and girl? Well, that would be giving the end away ...

20887

Contents

1   The worst Saturday night *ever*   1

2   Monday – school – yuck!   15

3   So ... could I trust Michelle?   29

4   I *had* to know what Mark looked like   39

5   Saturday night at my gran's – *great!*   47

6   We were going to meet up at last!   63

7   Sometimes I could *kill* my sister!   71

8   Meeting Mark – well, almost   77

9   So ... what did we think of each other?   83

Chapter 1

The worst Saturday night *ever*

It was one of those Saturday nights that will go down in history for *nothing at all*.

Here I was, 15 years old, long legs, shiny hair, straight teeth (thanks to years of *agony* from wearing a brace).

Here I was, sad to admit, installed on the sofa *at home*.

Everyone had gone to Matt's party – apart from me, of course. I wasn't invited.
No surprises there. It was only two days ago that I had dumped Nick. Or maybe he'd dumped me. Or maybe we'd dumped each other. He'd been acting weird with me for over a week.

I thought he might dump me, so I dumped him first. I thought I wouldn't feel so bad that way. But I did. I felt worse. Because now I was getting the creepy feeling that maybe he hadn't been going to dump me after all. I'd been really mean to him.

And now everyone was on his side. They were all having a *great* time at Matt's party. I could have been there right now if only I hadn't messed up with Nick.

I dragged a magazine off the floor. I'd flicked through it so many times I could tell you what was on every page.

There was no-one to go for a drink with. Nothing worth seeing at the local cinema. It was too wet to go for a walk. Even the cat looked fed up.

I lay on the sofa and zapped through the channels on TV, trying to get up enough energy to go down to the video shop and rent a movie.

That's when my mobile rang.

I jumped on it. The night might just turn out OK.

"This is the Abra-cab-dabra Cab Company calling."

The voice was young, male and fit, far too cool to come from a cab company.

"Uh-huh?" I said. I thought it might be some joker I knew.

"I'm sorry. Your cab's going to be late. Hold-up on the M—"

"Who is this?" I broke in.

"You *did* order a cab?"

"No."

"That *is* 07956 439 7778?" he asked.

"No. This is 07956 *5*39 7778."

"So you're not at 17 Elm Gardens?"

"No."

"Are you sure?"

"Of course I'm sure. I live here for God's sake."

"Sod it." He gave a sigh and the line was cut off.

Typical, I thought. *The one call of the night and it has to be a wrong number.*

I settled back on the sofa and tried to watch one of those spy thrillers that are

4

always on TV. Nothing made sense because I'd missed the first three minutes.

My sister stuck her head round the door.

"I'm off out now. What are you doing here?"

"What's it look like?"

"Where's Nick?" she asked, as if he might be under the sofa or something.

"He got run over by a bus."

"You mean he's dumped you?"

"No, I dumped him."

"About time, too. Frankly, he *was* sad." As always, my sister was so-ooo tactful.

"Thanks a lot."

"You could come for a drink with us if you *must*."

"It's not *that* bad."

The last time I'd been out with Jude and her darling boyfriend they left me in a dark corner of some club with a Coke and told me to watch Jude's leather jacket. It was so dark in that corner someone sat on me. I was invisible.

It wasn't until the front door slammed and I watched Jude's backside going down the street that I saw she'd borrowed my new denim hipster skirt without even asking. She was already too far away for me to shout at her. I went back to the sofa to plot how to pay her back.

Before I'd thought of anything lethal my phone rang again. I began to feel hopeful, but then ...

"Is that 07956 539 7778?"

"Oh, it's you again."

"Don't sound so thrilled."

"Wrong numbers aren't very thrilling."

"It's not a wrong number this time."

"Oh no?"

"Nope. I rang you because I want to know more about you."

"More about me?"

He put on an American drawl. "What's a girl like you doing *in* on a Saturday night?"

I waited for a moment. As far as I knew he might have eyebrows that met in the middle. He might be covered in zits. But then, as far as *he* knew, I might be, too.

Sometimes it's useful not knowing who it is you're talking to on the phone. I could be *anyone*.

"You see, I've got to get an early night. I've got a Calvin Klein shoot in the morning."

"Poor you," he said. "And on a Sunday, too."

"Umm. It's murder being a supermodel."

We were cut off by the voice of someone calling in on an intercom. They sounded as if they were being strangled under water. Then his phone cut out.

I stretched out on the sofa. Stuff Matt's party. Stuff Nick. There were loads of other guys in the world. Like this one. This one had made me laugh and I felt loads better.

I got back to my job of channel zapping.

I was really into a quiz show that I had found on one of the Sky channels. I'd got at least four questions right and would have won about £1,000 more than the guy on the show. He was rubbish.

Then my mobile rang again. I grabbed it. But it wasn't him. It was Michelle.

"Hi, Marie. You OK?"

I could hear the sounds of the party. Music was throbbing in the background. Michelle was my best friend. At least, kind of. I really didn't need her to feel sorry for me right now.

"I'm fine, thanks. Why?"

"I only wondered. What you up to?"

"Tonight?"

"Mmm."

I wasn't going to tell her I was sitting in front of the telly like some poor sad loser.

"This really cute guy keeps calling me up."

"That was fast work. Who? Do I know him?"

"No."

"You going to meet up with him?"

"Maybe later. He's working right now."

"Working? At this time? What does he do?"

I took a deep breath and tried to think of a really cool job someone could be doing on a Saturday night.

"He's a DJ."

"Really?" Michelle sounded deeply impressed. "Where?"

"All over the place. He does his own thing."

"Won't it be a bit late by the time you meet up?"

"Yeah, might give it a miss. What's the party like?"

"It's good. Yep, fine."

"Where are you? What's Nick doing?"

"I'm in the room with the coats and Nick's ... well, I think he's around somewhere."

"Is he on his own?"

"Umm ... not sure. Gotta go now."

She rang off. She sounded as if she was hiding something. *What*? I wondered.

Within minutes my phone rang again.

"Look, don't think I'm chatting you up or anything. I'm just desperate for *anyone* to talk to." It was that cab company guy again.

"Thanks *a lot*." I was about to put the phone down.

"Listen," he went on, "I'm shut up in this little black hole full of stale cigarette smoke. I'm freezing cold 'cos they turn the heating off at 9.30 p.m. I daren't even go for a pee in case someone phones. And no-one's phoned for a whole hour."

"How do I know you're not some pervert?"

"Do I sound like a pervert?"

"I dunno. What do perverts sound like?"

He did some silly heavy breathing down the phone.

I couldn't help giggling. "That was disgusting!"

"This place is a joke! It's got to be the worst cab company in the universe. None of the drivers know where anything is. I have to keep looking at maps for them."

"Why do you stick it?"

"Need the money. That is until my new single comes out."

"Oh yeah, sure."

"You don't believe me?"

"What's your band called?"

There was a moment's silence before he answered.

"A-Z," he said.

"I'll have to get down to Virgin and check you out. What kind of music?"

"Well, it's a kind of garage sound with a bit of house ..."

"Sounds as if *you're* going places," I teased.

I could hear a garbled voice in the background again and he cut in, "Hang on a second, I'll have to put you on hold ..."

He took ages. When he got back on the line he said, "Sorry about that. One of my drivers was trying to find the airport – in the middle of town."

We chatted on for a while after that.

His name was Mark and he didn't sound much older than me. And the more we talked, the more I liked the sound of him. I had this picture in my mind. Dreamy green eyes, tanned skin, just a hint of stubble perhaps. A kind of perfect mix of Brad Pitt and Becks rolled into one.

Chapter 2
Monday – school – yuck!

At school on Monday I met Michelle by the lockers.

She was kind of quiet about the party. I guessed she was trying to be kind. I mean, she wasn't going to rave on about a party I hadn't been invited to, was she?

"So, OK, what about this new guy of yours?" she asked.

"Well, I don't know him that well yet," I said.

"Does it mean that you and Nick are really over?"

"Oh yeah, we're over all right."

"Good," she said.

"Why good?"

"Well, I always said you weren't right for each other."

"Yes I know, but ..."

"Let's face it. You're too good for him, Marie," she said.

"Do you really think so?"

Michelle rolled her eyes. "*Yes.*"

The bell went for the next lesson at that point. She went off to her class, walking past a load of boys in a really obvious way.

I watched as the boys turned to check her back view. As Michelle knew they would. She swung her way down the corridor.

Typical! Her jeans were so low cut her knickers were showing.

Sometimes I wonder why she doesn't have "I'm free" tattooed over her backside.

****

He didn't ring on Monday night or Tuesday either. I checked loads of times to see if my mobile phone was charged. It was.

My sister Jude noticed and tackled me. She asked why I was so down in the mouth. I'd been having a go at her about my denim hipster skirt.

In the end she said she would lend me her new stretch black jeans in return. So I told her all about Mark. I felt I had to tell someone, in case he turned out to be a weirdo.

Jude looked hard at me. "So what does he talk about?"

I shrugged. "All sorts of things. Mainly the guys who drive his cabs."

"He sounds innocent enough."

"He is. He's really funny."

"Just don't meet up with him unless you've got someone with you, OK?"

"Of course not."

By Wednesday I was getting desperate.

My mobile bleeped while I was in the bath. Jude banged on the door. "Your mobile was bleeping – someone's sent you a message."

I leapt out of the bath and ran dripping to where I'd left it in the bedroom.

It was only a text from Michelle.

"Was that him?"

"No."

"Not exactly a phone menace, is he?" commented Jude.

****

By Thursday the weekend was starting to get closer again.

I didn't know if I could face another Saturday night with nothing planned and nothing likely to happen.

Michelle said she was going out with a load of people from school to a film and then McDonald's afterwards.

"Maybe I'll come along with you," I said.

She shook her head. "Nick's coming with us."

"But, really, there's no reason Nick and I can't be friends," I told her. "I mean, I miss him in a way. Maybe I should think about getting back with him. What do you think?"

"What did we agree, Marie? No going back," she said.

"I know. But I could just come along. And not sit with him or anything."

"I reckon it's too soon. You'll both feel really embarrassed."

"I suppose you're right. I don't want to spoil it for everyone. I won't come."

****

So, Saturday night found me all on my own again with the cat on the sofa. Mum and Dad were going to friends in the next street for supper.

20

"You can come if you like," said Mum as they left. "You could always do something with Sarah."

"With *Sarah?* She's *two* years younger than me, Mum."

"Oh, sorry," said Mum. "Only a thought."

I went into the kitchen and made myself baked beans on toast. Baked beans always make me feel better.

I carried the plate back to the sofa to eat in front of the TV. There was a travel programme on about Italy. It looked lovely and sunny and all the people in the street were so tanned and beautiful and wearing ultra-cool designer T-shirts and jeans.

Everyone in the whole world was having a great time except me.

I was just eating my first mouthful of beans on toast when my phone rang.

I jumped on it.

"Hi there. Is that Kate Moss? Or Cindy Crawford maybe?"

It was *him*. God, his voice was gorgeous.

"Hi," I replied through a mouthful of beans.

"What are you doing right now?" he asked.

I swallowed hard and the toast went down my throat in a great big lump. I wasn't going to tell him that, once again, I was sitting in front of the TV like some pathetic loser.

"Oh, eating. Errm – in a restaurant."

"Cool. What you eating?"

I stared at my plate. Nobody ate baked beans on toast in a restaurant.

"Spaghetti Bolognese. It's an Italian restaurant."

I turned up the sound on the TV for some background effects.

"Not eating alone, are you?"

"Course not. There are a load of us. My friend Michelle and some others."

"Cool. Sounds quite a party."

"Umm. How are you? How are your poor lost drivers?"

"Don't ask. We've got this new guy who's Polish. He doesn't speak any English. I'm having to start learning Polish."

The TV took a zoom at that point, right into the face of the female presenter. She started to talk about the back streets of Rome – in a very loud voice.

"Who's that?" Mark asked.

I fished for the remote and turned down the sound.

"My friend Michelle."

"She sounds kind of lively. Can I speak to her?"

My heart sank. If I said "no" he might start to suss that I was all alone.

"Errm, sure. Hang on a sec."

I started talking in what I think sounded just like the female presenter's voice.

"Hi. It's me, Michelle."

"Hello there."

"So you're a friend of Marie's?" I went on in my fake voice.

"Not really. In fact, I don't know her very well. I hear she's a model. What does she look like?"

I was starting to suspect that he knew what I was up to. But I couldn't stop now. I tried to think of my best points.

"Umm ... she's got brown hair and blue eyes and ... errm ... quite long legs. Look, I'll pass you back to her now."

"Hi, Mark. It's me, Marie, again," I said in my own voice. "Look, I gotta go. They're just serving some oranges stuffed with ice cream."

I rang off, my heart pounding. I was sure he knew it was me all along. This was so-oooo embarrassing. Now he'd never ring again.

I sat through a movie feeling really low, and then it got worse.

The next time my mobile rang, I answered it with a beating heart. But it wasn't him. It was Kath from my class.

I didn't get on that well with Kath. She liked to stir things. I wondered what she was ringing about. She should have been at the cinema with Michelle and the others.

"Aren't you at the film?" I asked.

25

"What film?" she replied.

"*Circle of Fire*. I thought you and Michelle and Nick and a load of you were going."

"Not that I know."

"Oh, that's odd. Michelle said ..."

"Look, Marie. I don't know if I should tell you this but ... but have you noticed anything about Nick and Michelle?"

"Nick and Michelle ...?" At last, the penny dropped. "You think they're going out together?"

"Well, they've gone to *Circle of Fire* together. Maybe you don't care, since you dumped him and everything."

"I don't," I lied.

"Well, that's OK then. I just thought you should know ..."

"Thanks a lot, Kath," I said. "That's really nice of you," and I rang off. I don't think she heard the sarcastic tone in my voice.

I'd gone hot and cold. I was so angry.

Why couldn't Michelle have told me herself? She was meant to be my best friend, wasn't she? And then I thought of how she'd listened to me moaning on about Nick. She'd been really kind.

Yes. *She* was the one who'd made me dump him in the first place. She must have fancied him herself all along.

I felt hot tears of anger pricking in my eyes. It wasn't losing Nick that hurt. It was all their lies. The two of them behind my back. The two of them must be out on their own together now.

I felt sick at the thought of it.

I went to bed early that night. But I couldn't sleep.

I didn't know how I could face Michelle on Monday at school.

Chapter 3

So ... could I trust Michelle?

The following Monday I stayed away from Michelle all morning. It wasn't until lunchtime, when we were side by side at the mirror in the cloakroom, that we had to talk.

I was doing my hair and she came closer to me.

"Hi," she said to my reflection.

"Hello," I said back in a really cool tone.

"You OK?"

"Enjoy the film on Saturday?" I asked.

Michelle gave a sigh, turned round and sat on the basins, staring at me.

"Yes, sure. Why?"

"Just wondered, that's all."

"Look, if it's about Nick, I can explain."

"Oh yes?"

"Marie, it's not my fault. You dumped him."

"Yes and whose idea was that?" I said, turning to her.

"Do you want him back?"

"*No.*"

"So what are we arguing about?"

"Who said we were arguing?" I said. I'd finished doing my hair and I slammed my brush back in my backpack and swept out.

I walked down the corridor, feeling really bad. Michelle had wanted to explain. But I hadn't given her a chance. I knew I was being really unfair. But she deserved it. Didn't she?

Later that day I bumped into Nick by the lockers. I hadn't spoken to him since the evening I'd dumped him. Or he'd dumped me. Or whatever. He'd been the one who'd been upset then.

He looked at me, not sure of what to say. Typical boy.

I slammed my books into my locker. He just stood there.

"What did you think of *Circle of Fire*?" I asked.

"Good. Yeah, it was cool. You ought to see it."

"I might do that," I said, and walked off with my head held high.

****

I didn't hear from Mark all week. I spent every evening up in my room doing homework. Or trying to. I was starting to understand how people in prison feel when no-one will speak to them. I didn't have Nick calling up any more. And I didn't have Michelle either. The worst thing about your ex going out with your best friend is that you lose both of them.

I couldn't talk to Jude about it because I knew she'd think the whole thing was stupid. And there was no way I was going to talk to Mum. She'd make a big thing of it all. I really needed to talk to someone who didn't know me, Michelle and Nick. I longed for Mark to ring. But he didn't.

By Friday night I couldn't bear it any longer. I looked up the Abra-cab-dabra Cab Company in the phone book.

Mark answered right away.

"Abra-cab-dabra Cab Company. Mark speaking. How can I help you?"

"Hi, Mark. It's me, Marie."

"Hi, Marie. You rang *me*. That's great. Unless you want a cab, of course."

"No, I just wanted to talk. Are you busy?"

"I've got a couple of drivers going round and round the ring road trying to find a way out. But apart from that I'm totally free. How about you? Had an interesting week? How was the Calvin Klein shoot?"

"Oh that, umm ..." The time had come to tell the truth. "I'm afraid, I'm not really a model."

"Oh. Shame. However, I'm not really in a band either."

"I didn't think you were."

"So, if you're not a supermodel, what do you really do?"

"If you really want to know, I'm still at school. Doing my GCSEs."

"Well, I only work here at weekends," Mark went on, "to get a bit of cash. I'm really doing my ASs."

"Really?!"

I knew then that I was so-oooo glad he was just an ordinary teenager at school, like me.

We talked for a while about what schools we went to. Every so often we had to stop talking so that Mark could help the cab drivers find their way around.

But, even so, we got to know an awful lot about each other. Like which films we liked and what music and stuff. And then we talked about our families. I found out that Mark didn't have a dad, he just lived with his mum. Which is why he had to work to earn his spending money. That made me feel pretty bad because Dad was always giving Jude and me handouts.

Mark came across as a bit lonely. But he didn't make a big deal of it. He was really easy to talk to – not like lots of other boys I've known.

I went to sleep that night with a good feeling inside. He'd promised to call me up the next night.

He did call me the next night. And the night after that. In fact, he called every night and we talked for an hour or so each time.

By the end of the week, we'd got to know so much about each other that we were starting to talk about things like which books we'd had when we were kids. (He had the *Hungry Caterpillar* and *Postman Pat* just like me.)

Then we talked about what colour fruit gums we liked. He liked the yellow and green ones – which I hate – I always go for the black and red ones. So you see – we were made for each other.

It was odd. People talk about love at first sight. But can you fall for someone you've never even seen?

We started talking about meeting up. But I think both of us were scared of this. He was the one who said it out loud.

"This may sound naff. But it's really bugging me. I want to know what you look like. But I don't want to meet up in case it spoils everything."

"But you do know what I look like. I told you. I mean, my friend Michelle did."

"No, but *really*."

"Me, too! I want to know what *you* look like."

"Why don't we send photos to each other?" he said.

"What if we don't like what we see?"

"I know I'll like what you look like."

"How can you be so sure?"

"I'll send you *my* photo, anyway. And if you like it, you can send yours back. How about that?"

"Hmm, maybe. But if I give you my address you might spy on me and see me for real and that would be cheating."

"OK, where shall I send the photo then?"

"Errm ... I know. You could send it to school. I'll get it that way."

"OK. It's a deal!"

Chapter 4

I *had* to know what Mark looked like

I couldn't think about anything else over the next few days.

I drove the school office mad. I kept coming to their door and asking if any post had come for me.

"What is it you're waiting for, Marie?"

"Oh just a ... errm, poster competition I entered," I made up.

On the Thursday morning one of the secretaries popped her head round the classroom door.

"It's come, Marie," she said, waving an envelope.

This was a really important moment. I wanted to be on my own when I opened it. I said thank you and went and hid in amongst the coats.

My hands were shaking as I slid out the photo.

And then I laughed out loud.

It was a photo of a baby. On the back was inscribed:

Mark, aged nine months.

I turned back to the front. He was a really great-looking baby with lots of mad curly hair and bright blue eyes.

That evening I looked through our family album and found a really funny photo of me aged six, grinning with my two front teeth missing. It had *Marie, Blackpool* and the date scrawled on the back by Dad.

I addressed it to Mark, c/o the Abra-cab-dabra Cab Company and dropped it in the post first thing the next day.

He rang me the following evening.

"That really wasn't fair," he said. "I still don't know what you look like."

"At least I was older in my photo than you were in the one you sent me."

"So what do you think of me so far?"

"Great hairstyle. How about me?"

"Yeah, cool. Except for one thing."

"What?"

"You have got front teeth, haven't you?"

"Yes, two of them."

"That's OK then."

****

At school that week I kept seeing Michelle and Nick together.

It was kind of odd not talking to them. These were the two people I knew best in the world, for goodness' sake.

I didn't mind any more about the two of them. Now I had Mark, I really didn't need Nick. All I wanted was for things to be back to normal and for us all to be friends again.

In the end, I decided to do something about it.

It was Friday, the end of the week. I wanted to see Michelle over the weekend. Maybe go shopping with her or something. I waited by her jacket at leaving time, ready to make up.

"Hi," I said. "You going home now?"

"Yes, why?"

"I just thought I might walk to the bus stop with you. It's stopped raining."

Michelle looked at me sideways. "OK."

She put her jacket on in silence and we went out together through the school gates.

"Look," I said, "I don't want to fall out with you over Nick."

"Nor do I," she said, turning to me. I could tell she meant it.

"Listen, Marie," she went on, "I didn't mean to go out with him. I really didn't. It's just that at the party we got talking. He was really down about being dumped.

"And I was saying stuff to make him feel better about it. And it sort of went from there ..."

"I guess he's kind of cute to start with," I said. "You'll learn."

"But you are over him. Aren't you?"

"Yeah. There's this other guy."

"The one who phones you up?"

"Umm."

"So you've met him?"

"Ermm, well, not exactly."

"You haven't?"

"No. It's hard to explain. We both think it would spoil things to meet up."

"Spoil things? Spoil what things?" she stared at me.

"Marie, are you trying to tell me you're *with* a guy you haven't even snogged? No, in fact, a guy you haven't even *seen*? That's *weird* if you ask me."

44

I'd stopped in my tracks.

"No, it's not. I know him better than loads of boys I've snogged. We talk about everything. It doesn't always have to be *physical* you know, Michelle.

"But I guess that's something you wouldn't understand."

Michelle had flung her backpack over her shoulder and was striding on ahead.

She'd taken what I'd said the wrong way. She always went further with boys than I did.

That's just the way she was.

"What I mean is, you wouldn't understand because you're not like me," I shouted after her.

My bus came round the corner just then and I had to run for it.

"You're right. I'm not like you.
I'm normal," she shouted back at me as I
climbed on board my bus.

Chapter 5

Saturday night at my gran's – *great!*

The next Saturday, Gran had invited us all over for a party. It was her 70th birthday. So we had to find some halfway decent clothes to wear.

I woke up with a bad feeling. I'd rowed with Michelle *again.* And I wasn't even going to be able to talk to Mark tonight because I'd be at Gran's.

Today was going to be one long pain.

When the time came, Jude and I had a bit of a row about who was going to wear her black stretch jeans. She won, of course. Even though she'd promised to lend them to me. So we weren't anywhere near ready when it was time to go.

I had to make do with the only other smart thing we had. Which was a knee-length skirt that was really baggy on me.

Mum and Dad were waiting in the car and Dad had hooted three times before Jude and I got in.

Jude was making a big fuss. "I mean, who could possibly want to start a party at six in the evening?" she was saying. So there was a bit of a mood in the car as we drove off.

Gran and Grandad's house is a few hours' drive away. It was raining and the car was really stuffy. The windows were all steamed up and I started to feel sick. So then, as always, Jude and I had a row because I wanted

48

the window open and she didn't. Then Dad started to get cross because Jude had her Walkman on and he could hear a tinny noise coming from it.

It was a typical family drive.

After we'd been driving for about an hour, my mobile rang. I could see it was Mark. I answered it.

"Hi. Look, I can't talk now. I'll try and call you later, OK?"

Jude had noticed the call and taken her Walkman off.

"Was that him?" she hissed.

"Who?" asked Mum.

"No-one," I said.

"*No-one* doesn't call you on your mobile," said Dad.

"Is that proper English?" asked Mum.

"Come on, Marie. Cheer our boring old lives up. Who was it?" Dad asked.

"Maybe she doesn't want to say," said Mum, turning round and smiling at me. "Maybe it's someone new."

"Oh, boyfriend, is it?" said Dad. "Is it that Nick chap?"

Jude gave a groan. "*Daa-d!* Get a life. You must know that Nick and Marie have broken up. Everyone else in the entire universe does."

"It must be someone new, then," said Mum in a bright voice, trying to keep the peace. "Is he at school with you?"

"No. And don't get excited about him," I said. "I hardly know him."

"Oh? So why does someone you hardly know ring you up on your mobile?" asked Dad.

He was kind of teasing but I didn't want him to go on.

"If you *must* know, it was a wrong number."

"It can't have been," said Mum. "You said you'd call him back."

"Can you all please leave me alone! It was a wrong number the first time and then we got talking, that's all. I don't even know him."

Mum had turned right round in the front seat.

"You mean you're talking to someone you don't know?"

"Well yes, no, I mean, I kind of know him now."

"How long has this been going on?"

"Three weeks," said Jude.

I glared at her.

Dad had slowed down. He was looking at me in the car's rear-view mirror.

"Your mum's right. You can't talk to people you don't know on the phone. He could be anyone."

"It's just some boy, for God's sake. He's still at school."

Dad pulled in and stopped the engine. Mum and Dad were both staring at me now.

Suddenly World War Three had broken out inside the car.

"Does he know our address?" demanded Dad.

"Of course not."

"Well, that's a blessing," said Mum.

"This will have to stop right away, Marie. Do you hear?" Dad said.

"But we were only talking on the phone."

"No, I'm sorry. I'm not having it. You'll have to change your number."

"But, Dad ..."

"No buts, Marie."

"But all my friends have got this number."

"I don't care who's got your number. It's *got* to be changed."

"It's not fair," I said.

Mum broke in. "What if Marie tells him they can't call each other up any more and promises us that she won't talk to him again?"

Dad shrugged. "I suppose that'll be a start."

"We want you to promise, Marie," said Mum.

"Do I really have to?"

"Yes," said Dad. "Or else – new number."

"But I'll have to call him to tell him ..."

"Just that one call. Then that's it."

"Come on, we're going to be late for the party if we don't get a move on," said Jude. "And then Gran'll be upset."

"I'm listening, Marie," insisted Dad.

"OK, I promise," I said.

Dad started up the engine again. He drove off but I could see, even by looking at the back of his neck, that he was angry.

You wouldn't think that the back of someone's neck could tell you so much.

We all sat fed up and in silence for the rest of the journey. Jude's Walkman was ticking all the way and I felt *really* sick.

I was going to have to ring Mark later and tell him he was never to call me again. How could parents be so unfair?

****

My uncles and aunts and all my little
cousins were there at Gran's. There were so
many of us that Gran had got people in to do
the food.

Everything on the table was all bright and
shiny and covered in jelly stuff. It looked
fantastic but tasted odd. I didn't feel like
eating anyway, what with the drive and
having to make that phone call and
everything.

"You're looking a bit pale, Marie," said
Gran. She turned to Mum. "Those girls of
yours don't eat enough," she said. (She
always says that.)

I couldn't get away from the party until
we'd finished eating and Gran had blown out
her candles. There really were 70 of them.
It took her ages.

Then I went and hid in her spare bedroom
with my mobile.

Gran's spare bedroom is where Jude and I used to stay when we were little. The curtains and chairs are all flowery and there are two single beds with pale pink sicky-looking covers.

Gran always has a few of our old reject teddies tucked into the beds. As if, one day, by magic, Jude and I are going to be little again and come back and sleep there. That room makes me feel depressed.

I punched Mark's number into my mobile.

He answered, as always, with, "Abra-cab-dabra Cab Company. Mark speaking. How can I help you?"

"Hi. It's me."

"What's up?"

"Something really awful's happened."

Mark knew I was going to Gran's birthday party.

"God, your gran hasn't swallowed a candle, has she?"

"No. It's nothing like that. It's just that Mum and Dad have found out about us talking and they say we've got to stop."

"What? Stop talking?"

"On the phone like this."

"Do your parents belong to some weird religion or something?"

"No. I know it sounds as if they're strict, but it's the way they got to know about you. I didn't mean to but I let out that it all started with a wrong number."

"So-o?"

"Dad seems to think you're an axe murderer."

"Oh, I see."

"I mean, I know you're not and everything …"

"Thanks …" Mark didn't say anything for a bit. Then, "What if we just keep talking anyway?" he went on.

"I can't, they made me promise. You're not to call me. And this is the last time I can call you, ever."

"Oh."

There was another silence.

"That's it, then."

"Yes," I said. I felt awful.

"We'll just have to meet up."

My heart flipped over.

"What?" I said.

"Well, your dad didn't make you promise not to meet me, did he?"

"No ... no, I suppose he didn't."

"OK. Right. So if this is the last time we can talk on the phone we'd better arrange something now."

"Yes," I said. Things were moving faster and faster. My head was spinning.

"Right," he said. "We need to meet somewhere public. To be on the safe side. I don't want to get date raped."

I tried not to giggle. "But when?"

"The sooner the better. Doing anything tomorrow afternoon?"

"Nothing important."

"OK. Now, where?"

I thought hard.

I knew Mark lived on the other side of town. The best bet was to meet midway. Which was even better because it was well out of the way of my parents. We needed somewhere public but where I wasn't going to bump into a load of people I knew.

Suddenly, I remembered a place we used to go to for a treat after going to the museum.

"There's a little café over the road from the museum. That's open on Sundays. We could meet there."

I gave Mark the name of the place and we arranged to be there at four.

There was a funny sound on the other end of the line.

"What's that noise?"

"Just sharpening my axe."

"Hang on. How will I know it's you?"

"Don't worry, you'll know." He rang off.

I clicked my mobile shut.

I had to think fast.

What should I wear? I'd have to wash my hair in the morning. Was there any hair gel left? Should I wear jeans? Or a skirt to show off my legs?

I met Jude on the landing. She'd come to find me.

"Mum and Dad are getting ready to go," she said. "So, have you rung him?"

"Yes," I said. I tried to look upset.

"You don't look too cut up about it."

"It was only someone I spoke to on the phone. Would you be?"

"Not likely," she replied in a typical Jude tone of voice. Then she looked at me oddly. "You did call him, didn't you?"

"Yes."

"And you did say you couldn't call each other up any more?"

"*Yes.*"

"That's OK then."

Chapter 6

We were going to meet up at last!

The next morning I woke early with butterflies in my stomach. It took me a second or so to remember why. Yes, today I was going to meet Mark.

I spent ages in the shower. After that I rubbed in lots of body lotion and did my nails. In fact, I gave myself a total body makeover. Dad hammered on the bathroom door three times before I was out.

"I thought you'd decided to stay in there for ever," he said.

"Sorry."

Mum was in the kitchen cooking breakfast. She stared at me when I walked in.

"Hey, what are you doing up so early? Have aliens invaded and stolen your bed?"

"I just felt like getting up early for once, that's all."

She gave me a hug. I could tell she felt mean about yesterday's scene. But she couldn't go against Dad.

"So, what do you fancy? Special breakfast? French toast with cinnamon sugar?"

"No thanks. I'll just have juice and an apple."

She looked at me from across the kitchen.

"What are you up to today?"

"Oh, nothing much. Meeting up with someone around 4 o'clock."

"Is that Michelle?"

"Umm."

"That's nice. She hasn't been round lately. Everything OK?"

"Don't pester, Mum."

"Sorry. Want a yogurt with that apple? There's a black cherry one, I think."

"OK." I sat down and ate the yogurt to keep her happy.

Dad came in, smelling of shaving foam.

He looked at my apple and yogurt. "That all you're having?"

"That's all I ever have, Dad."

"Want to come out this afternoon? I've got to drive over to Harding's to pick up some fence posts. We could have a walk in the forest."

I shook my head.

"Sorry. Already doing something."

"Can't you do whatever it is some other time? We haven't had an afternoon out together in ages."

I could tell he wanted to make up with me.

"No, can't change it. Sorry."

"That's a turn up. I thought you kids always changed everything at the last minute," Dad said in a grumpy way, as he sat down in front of the plate of eggs and bacon Mum passed him.

"Well, I can't change this," I said, a bit too fast.

"I'm sure Michelle would understand," Mum said. "Or she could go with you ..."

"No. She wouldn't want to."

I felt myself going hot. I felt such a liar.

Mum and Dad looked at each other.

"I think I'll finish my breakfast in front of the TV if that's all right," I said, and carried my plate into the sitting room.

I sat staring blankly at a load of cartoons on telly. I wasn't even watching them. I hated going behind Mum's and Dad's backs. Oh, why did parents have to make everything so difficult? Now I'd said I was meeting up with Michelle when I wasn't. What if Michelle came round? Which wasn't very likely. But she might feel bad about our row and come round to make up. That was just the sort of thing she would do.

I was going to have to call her. I dialled her number. Her phone rang for ages.

"Who's that?" came a grumpy voice.

Oh no, I thought, *I've woken her up*.

"It's me."

"Do you know what time it is?"

"Sorry, I didn't think. I was up early."

"Am I wrong or is it Sunday?"

"You're right. I'm really sorry to call so early."

"So?" She still sounded mad at me.

"Look, listen. Just in case you were thinking of dropping by my place today ..."

"Me dropping by? No, why?"

"Well, don't, that's all."

"Thanks a lot."

"No. Don't get me wrong. I won't be in, that's all."

"Oh?"

"So see you on Monday, OK?" I was about to ring off.

"Hang on, Marie. Last time I saw you, you just about said I was sex-mad. Now, you wake

68

me up at dawn on a Sunday and tell me that I *can't* come round to your place – which I wasn't going to anyway. What's going on? Where are you going?"

"I'm just meeting someone, that's all."

At once she was wide awake. "It's Nick, isn't it?"

"*No.*"

"I knew it. He's been acting really odd all week. He said he couldn't see me this afternoon. It all adds up."

"No, it doesn't. It's just Nick. He's like that. With every girl. I did warn you."

"You're getting back together, aren't you?"

"*No!*"

"Then who are you meeting?"

"OK. I might as well tell you. It's Mark ..."

"The guy who calls you up?"

"Yes."

"So-ooo, going to get to know him better, are you?"

"Well, that's the plan."

"Great. What are you going to wear?"

Which got us into one of our endless chats about what to wear.

It ended with Michelle saying, "Call me up the second you're alone and tell me what he's like. Promise!"

So even if meeting Mark turned out to be really bad news, one good thing had happened. Michelle and I were friends again.

Chapter 7

Sometimes I could *kill* my sister!

I spent the rest of the morning trying hard to work out what to wear. I took every single thing out of my wardrobe and tried it on. I even went through the dirty washing basket and put two of my best T-shirts on a quick wash cycle. I went through smart-casual, smart-smart, casual-casual, extra-casual down to really-don't-care and back again.

In the end I decided that the only thing I really wanted to wear was my new denim hipster mini-skirt. This would show off my best point which was my legs. And it was nicely casual-casual without being too don't-care. But the skirt had *vanished*. Anyone who has ever had a sister won't need telling where.

I crept into Jude's room. The blinds were still tight shut and I could tell by the lump under the duvet that she was dead to the world. I decided not to put the light on. If you wake Jude first thing in the morning, it can be *scary*. I groped my way through all the piles of clothes on the floor. Then I went through all the clothes hanging over her chair. There was only the wardrobe left. Inside the wardrobe was even darker than the room. You can't see denim in the dark. Finding a small hipster mini-skirt is virtually impossible. I was just feeling my way through her million coat hangers when a kind of landslide of them slid sideways and crashed onto the floor.

The lump in the bed split apart. Like the incredible hulk appearing, Jude rose up out of the duvet.

"What are you doing in my room?"

"I was just looking for—"

"You're going through my clothes!"

"I'm only looking for—"

"If I find you've stolen anything, I'll—"

This was too much. It was her who stole my stuff for goodness' sake. I had every right to get my own clothes back. I made this point and made it loudly. At which point, Jude shouted back. Then she threw a pillow at me. And I knocked her chair over.

Dad's shadow loomed in the doorway.

"What's going on?" he demanded.

"Marie came into my room without even knocking."

"She took my clothes without even asking," we both said together.

"Stop. One at a time."

In the end, I did find out what had happened to my mini-skirt. Last weekend Jude had taken it, along with a load of her clothes, to her friend Liz's, so that they could dress up together to go clubbing.

"And I didn't wear it anyway," Jude said at last.

"So where is it?" asked Dad.

"It must still be at Liz's. Unless it *walked* home," snapped Jude. "Now can I get some sleep?"

My blood was boiling.

"Dad – that's so unfair."

"So why is this item of clothing so important?" he asked.

"I wanted to wear it this afternoon."

"Well, wear something else," said Dad. He'd had enough. He stomped off.

"So what *is* so important about this afternoon?" asked Jude, as soon as he was gone.

"Nothing."

"You're meeting *him*, aren't you?"

"No!"

Jude looked hard at me from her bed.

"Yes, you are. I can tell when you're covering something up."

"No, you can't. Anyway, they didn't say anything about not *seeing* him."

"I just hope you're meeting him somewhere public."

"Very. The café by the museum, if you must know. The one we used to go to with Dad."

"Well, I suppose you can't come to much harm there. Unless you choke to death on cake."

"Pl-ease don't tell Mum and Dad."

"I'll think about it."

"I'll do anything ..."

"I suppose Dad was being rather heavy," she said.

"Thanks, Jude. I owe you one."

"Good. Because Liz ironed the mini-skirt with a too hot iron and it's trashed."

(*So that was why she was being so nice.*)

Jude turned over in bed and pulled up the duvet. "You can borrow my black stretch jeans if you like."

I stood and stared at her for a long time. If she dared tell anyone I was meeting Mark she was dead meat.

Chapter 8

Meeting Mark – well, almost

So I wore Jude's new stretch black jeans to meet Mark. They were a bit long so I wore my boots with heels which made me look taller. And I took ages over my make-up. I tried to creep past the kitchen but Mum came out just at the wrong time.

"You look nice," she said. She saw I'd made an effort. "Have a good time."

"Yes, thanks. I won't be late," I said as I slunk out of the front door.

On the bus I started to worry about meeting Mark. What if he was really gross? What if his baby curls were wild, greasy dreadlocks? I was going to be so-oooooo embarrassed. I mean, he was a really nice guy. I didn't want to hurt his feelings.

So I thought of a better plan. I would get to the café a quarter of an hour late and have a good look round. If I didn't like the look of anyone in it, I would simply slip away. That way nobody's feelings would be hurt.

So I hung around in the street outside for a full 20 minutes. At exactly 4.20 I went into the café and stood in the doorway. I looked round the room to see if there was any boy that could be Mark. There wasn't. In fact, there was no-one younger than 60 in there. So, in spite of the fact I was late, I must have got there first.

I chose a table in the window and ordered a hot chocolate. From where I sat, I could see everyone who was coming up to the door of the café. If I needed to, I could make a quick getaway.

I wished I could stop the feeling of panic every time some guy who was about Mark's age came round the corner. There were loads of them. Tall, short, fair, dark, Italian-looking, hands in or out of pockets, in jeans, in chinos, leather jackets, raincoats, even one guy in shorts (not him, p-lease). I'd watch to see if they'd a) cross the road, b) stop at the bus stop, c) go into the newsagent's, d) stare in through the café window. No-one came into the café. The nearest any of them came was staring in through the window. An hour crept by and my heart sank. If Mark was held up, why didn't he ring?

In the end, even though I didn't want to, I dialled the Abra-cab-dabra Cab Company.

A foreign voice answered.

"Hello, is Mark there?"

"Mark? No, luv. He had something on."

"Oh, right. Have you got his mobile number?"

"No, sorry. Don't think he's got one. I could give him a message when he comes in."

"No. Thanks. Doesn't matter."

I rang off. Just my luck. He must be the only boy left on the planet without a mobile. Where was he? I stared sadly out of the window. It had started to rain. Why hadn't he come? And then I had an awful thought. Maybe he *had* come. Maybe he'd been one of the guys who'd looked through the window and seen me. And he'd decided *he* didn't like the look of *me*. Then he'd gone away.

It was five o'clock. It was too late for him to turn up now. Glumly, I paid for my hot chocolate and went back round the corner to the bus stop.

It was a Sunday and there were loads of young and happy people around. They were nearly all in pairs. Most of them were holding hands and stuff.

I waited for ages and then, at last, a Number 22 bus came along. That's when my mobile rang.

"Hi! Marie!"

It was *him*.

My mouth had gone dry and the palms of my hands were wet.

"Where are you?"

"In a phone box. It was the only one I could find working."

"Where?"

"Outside the café. I went in but you must've left. I'm so-oo sorry. One of my drivers crashed his cab and I had to sort out the hospital and insurance and everything."

"But that's where I am. Just outside the café, too."

"You can't be. Where?"

"In a bus. But it's just leaving."

"What bus?"

"The 22."

"The 22? I can see it from here. Look out of the bus window and wave!"

"Wave where?" I looked across the street. That's when I saw – oh-my-god – this guy in a phone box waving like crazy and *holding a massive axe*.

The lunatic. The total mad idiot. I shook my head at him and waved back.

He was pretty nice-looking as a matter of fact. I mean not totally handsome or anything but he had a wicked smile. I just prayed he liked the look of me.

Chapter 9

So ... what did we think of each other?

He liked me. Well, I think he did. When I got off the bus and we met up at last we spent two whole hours in the café.

I mean, I don't think either of us was quite as fantastic as we had thought. For a start, he was a bit shorter than me. But then I had high heels on that day. And he said I'd put on loads too much make-up that first time we met. And I thought he had a really gross haircut. (Not his fault, his mum cut it.)

But since we've been going out together, we've kind of sorted those things out. And now he's met Michelle and Nick. In fact, we've all been out together. Even Jude says that he's not that bad for a friend of mine. So he might drop round at my place sometime and Mum and Dad can meet him, *maybe*.

But, to tell the truth, he'll never quite live up to the guy I fell for. That impossibly perfect person who rang me on a wrong number. But then I guess, looking at it from his point of view, nor will I.

Barrington Stoke would like to thank all its readers for commenting on the manuscript before publication and in particular:

Helen Adair	Megan Geddes	Nicky Mustoe
Lizzie Alder	L. Goddard	Richard Needham
James Barton	Louis Gordo	Tom O'Connor
Shaun Brown	Sylvia Gorman	Chesney Osborne
Mrs M. Browning	Hazel Gregory	Zoe Pattenden
Jodie Burling	Alla Hassan	C. Penhorwood-Richards
Martin Callow	Gavin Horgan	Melissa Reid
Ryan Clair	Davina Kenny	Rosemary Richey
Jack Clarke	Chris Leydon	Emily Smyth
Tarnya Coleshill	Scott Lofthouse	Owen Thomas
Suzanne Cooper	Ann MacDonald	Beverley Ward
Jennifer Cotton	Eve McCowat	Amy West
Stacey Crofts	S. McGovern	Yolanda Westall
R. Cunningham	C. McLay	Stuart White
Pedro Da Silva	Jordan Marshall	Melissa Witham
Natasha Davidson	Natasha Mason	Sue Wood
Jennifer Edge	C. Melton	Yasmin Yafai
Laura Esberger	Juber Miah	
Ann Falch	Hannah Mitchell	

Become a Consultant!

Would you like to give us feedback on our titles before they are published? Contact us at the address below – we'd love to hear from you!

Barrington Stoke, Sandeman House, Trunk's Close,
55 High Street, Edinburgh EH1 1SR
Tel: 0131 557 2020 Fax: 0131 557 6060
E-mail: info@barringtonstoke.co.uk
Website: www.barringtonstoke.co.uk

If you loved this book why don't you read ...

Text Game

by Kate Cann

ISBN 1-842991-48-5

"... it's like I'm frozen, my mind's somewhere else ... that voice in my head is telling me to ask him about the texts, but I can't. I'm so scared. Scared he'll lie, scared of the truth."

Everything's going great in Mel's life. And the best bit's Ben. He's gorgeous, he's fun and great to be with – she can't believe he's going out with her. Then she starts getting nasty text messages. They say Ben's playing with her. They say he's going to dump her. They say he's seeing someone else. Are they just from some jealous nutcase, like her friend Lisa says? Or are they telling the truth?

You can order *Text Game* directly from our website at **www.barringtonstoke.co.uk**